I0688546

PARALLELED

BOND

PARALLELED

BOND

Stephanie Hansen

HYPOTHESIS

BOOKS

ISBN 978-1-7350423-3-6

1 2 3 4 5 6 7 8 9 10

Printed in the U.S.A.
First printing, 2020

The text type was set in Perpetua and Times New Roman.

Cover design by inkE Cover Designs

For my husband, Nate,

You are my rock. Without you it would be

hell to see some things through.

∞   ∞

ANAPHASE

"Please let them be okay." If I had known I would be chanting this phrase over and over again, I don't believe I would have ever set out on this mission. If I had known that my entire world would change in just a matter of months, would I have taken the job at the haunted house? If I had been given a heads up about my DNA being different, would I have lived a different life?

I don't know; those are not options for me now. We're too far in. We are inches away from saving many lives. We can do this. I know we can. I just don't know what it will cost us. I have no clue how I'm going to find the dough to pay. The odds seem stacked up against us. Is that because it is impossible to accomplish what we want to, or is it because we've gotten too close?

REJECTED

As I wait for the grassy pad, a shadow approaches me. Instead of the scent of fresh-cut grass, I smell rosewater. What's going on? I've never met a shadow while travelling from one world to the other. My vision of everything is blurry. I can't make out a single thing. Maybe it was more than a shadow, but I'm unable to make out details right now. My nerves begin to fray. It feels like someone's taking a nail and scraping it up my arm. Something's interfering with my travel. It's so quiet wherever I'm trapped. Is this some kind of portal? A space between Earth and the Stranded Coil I've never stopped before? It's difficult to concentrate as I try to see if I can feel my father's presence anywhere nearby. Am I too late? Has he already sacrificed himself? I'm trying to make my final visit to the

Other World, leaving Josh and everyone behind, to save him, but I feel more lost now than I ever have. I don't understand what's going on at all. Why am I not sitting near the beach feeling the sand particles' emotions?

"Because I made a promise to your father, that's why," a voice from nowhere exclaims. I know that voice. No wonder I smelled rosewater. Slowly her image appears. The eyes are dark as charcoal, yet glow just like charcoal does after you light it. She has an infectious smile that makes me laugh even though I can see a lecture behind it.

"Grandmother, what are you doing? I have to save him." It feels strange to talk here. Whatever this place is, I hope I don't have to stay long. My grandmother's presence is comforting, but I still feel as though I'm on the brink of an anxiety attack. The feeling of having a physical form is leaving me. If it weren't the palms of my hands

3

would be sweating. Instead, I feel static like we're in an electrical field.

"No Austria, you don't. You're his child, and he wants you to enjoy life."

How am I supposed to enjoy life when it's ripping my father away from me yet again? My chest clenches. I'm unable to take a breath.

"What's going to happen to him?" I manage to gasp out.

"He's taking Adam to Heaven with him. I'm pretty sure, once they meet the celestial gate, that Adam will be turned away. There's only one place he'll be able to go then. I'm sure you know where that is. I'm glad because I don't want to spend my eternity with a man like that."

"Are you saying that you and Father will be in Heaven?" I'm able to breathe and talk again because now I know there's a way to see him again even if he goes through with this plan. I begin to feel the spinning. Maybe if I keep Grandmother talking, I'll be forced to the Other World anyway. Then I'll be closer to him, or at least closer to the stairs.

"Yes, dear, it's where we belong."

"I just got you guys back."

"Most people aren't given such a chance. Please treasure the moments we've had together as I will and enjoy your life."

I understand what Grandmother is telling me, but I'm not happy about it. I imagine my father and grandmother in front of Heaven's gates. I can hear trumpets sounding their arrival. The perfect symphony causes goosebumps to form on my legs. I can't do anything to keep them from moving on. She's preventing me from travelling to the Other World. The spinning is beginning to cease. Maybe if I come from another angle.

"How are we going to continue the fight without you guys around?"

"We have a team up here. You've met them. Plus we're adding a new leader. One you're very familiar with."

"Who's the new leader?"

"Why it's me, Austria." I know that voice too. It's the voice that's comforted me every day of my life. What's my mother doing here? I didn't think this could be possible. What does my grandmother mean about my mother being the leader in the Other World?

"Mother, how are you communicating with us? You're not an Altered Helix."

"Well actually, Marie is. Your father realized she was before she did and hid it from her. He didn't let anyone from the Other World contact her. He wanted her to be able to live a normal life with you. He wanted to protect her from our enemies. If she didn't know she was an Altered Helix, how would they?" my grandmother answers. How can that be? Why had she not noticed the shadows at the haunted house? Then I remember she's a couple years younger than my father and the Altered Helix abilities might not have kicked in for her until after that experience.

"She's right. I didn't know. Your father just contacted me before he left to take Adam to the next world. It was so amazing to see him again. I love him just as much as I did when he was home. I wish I had more time with him but, Austria, I understand what he's trying to do. It's a noble cause, and I also want you to have a normal life."

"So you're going to be in the Other World. You're the new leader. I'm losing my whole family." The air I'm breathing thickens, and I feel my airway constricting. The spinning I feel isn't from the Other World this time. It's from lack of oxygen to my brain.

FAREWELL

"Calm down, Austria," my mother says delicately.

"What am I going to do without you? You and I have spent every holiday together. I don't want to lose that. And I want to have some family at my wedding. I want my mother to be there when I have children."

"We'll still be able to talk, darling. Most Altered Helixes are allowed multiple visits to the Other World but, as the leader, I'm going to be anchored here. My abilities acclimated during the past decade and so I only need one visit. Hey, everything is going to be okay. I feel complete with my responsibilities here and one day, many years from now, you will be too. You'll see."

"Plus, your children will more than likely have different DNA too since both your parents do, Austria. They'll be able to meet your mother." This comes from my grandmother.

She's right. They're both right, but I don't want them to be. My hands are furiously shaking. Why is it that my mother only gets one visit? My grandmother had multiple at her age. It's because she's the leader. I wonder if Altered Helixes can manipulate that? Again I'm fraught with an apprehension that causes jitters. Then it dawns on me. If my children have Altered Helixes too, they'll be in danger if we don't stop these people. I'm about to say something when I'm interrupted.

"It's time. I have him." That's my father's voice.

"Father, I don't want you to go. I love you."

"I have to, honey. I love you too."

"What the hell do you people think you're up to?" Adam's here too.

"Adam, you're deranged. and the group and plans you've put together need to be stopped," my father says.

"You're just upset that you didn't come up with them first."

"No. I do not want a dictatorship in the Other World, just as I had not wanted one on Earth."

"There's no way you can stop what I have in place. I never lose."

"You'd be surprised what we have in place ourselves."

My father turns to us and gives us all hugs. When he hugs me, I don't want to let go. I breathe in the smell of his aftershave one last time. He pulls away and kisses my forehead.

"I'll always be watching over you. One day, many years from now, we'll be together again. I promise."

He turns to Adam. "Come on. I'll show you everything we've been up to."

My father takes Adam's arm. As Adam tries to free himself, everything changes.

10

Instead of being in the void I'd been, I'm on my knees on the floor in my room. Now I'm watching them just through a vision, similar to how I first saw my father at the haunted house before any of this outlandishness began. Before I found out I was different. Before I found out we were in danger.

They're on the grassy pad by the beach, and Adam looks disoriented. Altered Helixes can read thoughts in the Other World, but Mutated Altered Helixes cannot. My father points up the stairs. The stairs that lead to Heaven that he stopped me from ascending too early.

"Matt and Ed are up there," my father tells Adam.

"Why do I care if they're up there? I have a bit more on my hands to deal with," Adam says.

"Because they've switched sides, and they're stopping all of your work. I told you they would. In fact, they're almost done. I told you we'd win."

Adam's face is twisted in anger. "We'll see about that," he says and then takes the first step. Once his foot touches the stair, it's as if a magnetic pull takes him the rest of the way. His facial muscles have relaxed, and he looks as if he just received a massage and doesn't have a care in the world.

My father and grandmother take each other's hands. They look back at my mother and me and blow us kisses. We both simultaneously blow kisses back. Then they take a step too. The light that surrounds them brightens. The things they have done all these years when I didn't even know they were around simply amaze me. How they've been trying to protect me all along. I had felt empty and lonely at times but maybe, deep down, I had always known they were there. They've always been supporting me and cheering me on. When I looked in the stands to see if anyone was watching my school events, I should have known they were there in spirit. No world could hold back their love.

The brilliant light isn't the only thing clouding my vision. Tears are streaming down my cheeks. I cannot swallow. This isn't the way it was supposed to be. My mother, so pretty, withstood an enormous amount of pressure raising me and keeping a secret in order to protect me. Now she's making a completely selfless move. She'll be in a world that's totally new to her. I see enormous strength in her that I never noticed before.

"Everything's going to be okay, Austria. I'm just an email away if you ever need anything," my mother says.

It all fades away—the stairs, the grassy pad, and my mother's face. I'm back in my room. Everything looks the same. The lamp's still off with the shade askew. My note on my pillow is still right where I put it. My dirty laundry spread throughout the room hasn't moved an inch. My *The Catcher in the Rye* book is still on my nightstand with a gum wrapper for a bookmark. But everything has changed.

Nothing's the same. Not without my father back in my life and my mother gone. I'm alone, and now it's my responsibility to make this a safe place for my future children and all Altered Helixes. It feels as though I've aged a decade in weeks. It feels as though everything's spiraling out of control.

HEARTBREAK

I crumple to the floor sobbing. I'm not just crying now. It's one of those intense, wretched sobs that shake your entire body. I pull my knees into my chest trying to comfort myself. I try to see some way out or some way to make things right, but I know there's nothing. Nothing will ever make this pain go away. My body begins convulsing, and I can't make it stop. I see Josh's face in front of me but cannot hear what he's saying. I'm not surprised that my wailing woke him. I feel him wrap his arms around me and lift me to a sitting position. Even with a cast, he does this with ease. His lips move, and he looks in my eyes. I can't move a muscle. It feels as though I can't even blink. I'm frozen. I'm like a statue of misery.

He turns his head away from me and opens his mouth wide. He's screaming something. The vein on the side of his forehead's bulging out. Then Tiff's shaking me. She's also saying something, but I don't hear her. Luke grabs a flashlight and shines it in my eyes. He's checking my vitals. I feel him touch my wrist with his thumb and forefinger. Then he and Josh pick me up and put me on the bed. That's when Josh sees the note. I see him open it and read it. His eyes move back and forth across the page. His facial expressions change over and over again as he reads. I wish I could wrap my arms around him. I wish I could talk and explain. None of those things are available to me. He squeezes the note in his hand and says something to Tiff and Luke.

Tiff grabs my phone and unlocks it. She says something to me, but I still don't hear her. Am I going to remain in this deaf and mute state of paralysis forever? Was it the portal that did this to me, or is this how everyone is when they lose their entire family?

Tiff shows me the screen. She has my father's email up. She points it at me and looks like she's asking me something, but I still can't hear. Then she turns it back to herself. She's touching the screen, but I have no idea what she's doing. What if she's deleting his message, the last message from my father? I try to will my body to move so I can grab the phone. I swear I'm flexing my muscles in my arm hard enough to lift fifty pounds, but my arm doesn't even budge. Then she turns the phone back to me. There's a message from my mother. Before I can read it, she turns it back to herself.

A tear rolls down her cheek, and she hugs me. Luke holds my hand. Josh is looking at the phone now. He's pacing back and forth. I wonder what was in my mother's message. Did she talk about everything? Then Josh stops and drops to his knees. He looks at me, and I can see understanding in his eyes. We're both without family in this world now. We're all each other have. He walks over to the bed and says something to Luke and Tiff. They get up and leave the room. Josh sits down next to me. He smells like the woods. I wish I could be hidden away somewhere in the woods. Lost in a cabin with him away from society and away from where everyone else has a family.

He picks me up and walks to the bathroom. He sets me down on the floor mat. It's one of those mats with extra padding. It feels like I'm sitting on a cloud. More feeling is coming back. Then I remember my father and grandmother walking up the stairs towards the clouds. A tear springs through my eyelashes. Josh wipes it away with his fingertip. Then he turns the water on. I can hear it hitting the tub. My hearing's returning too. I'm not sure I'm ready to be back. My father will never be back. Why should I?

Josh begins to brush my hair. I look in his eyes. They've always made me think of clear blue water. It reminds me of the grassy pad next to the beach I was supposed to land on instead of going to a portal and watching my loved ones being taken from me. Multiple tears flow down my cheeks now. I begin to shake and writhe in agony again. Josh strips my pajamas off of me, picks me up, and puts me in the water. It's warm. It calms me. His arms soothe me despite the cast and awkward moves it requires in order for him to keep it dry.

"Everything's going to be fine, Austria. Stay with me."

I focus on my muscles again. I'm able to move my hand. Hallelujah. I put my hand on his forearm as he scoops water with a cup and pours it on me. I see a very small movement in his facial muscles. He's hiding a smile. I actually want to smile back. I can feel the bubbles he must have added to the bath without me noticing pop as I move. Josh lathers soap and rubs it on my skin. Every place he scrubs takes a little bit of the pain away. He helps me lower myself to wet my hair. I can feel him lathering shampoo in my hair. For a second, I feel whole again. It quickly fades as I think about how the bath water reminds me of the beach near the grassy pad. The tears return. I try to pull myself down. I want to submerge my whole head below the water.

"Oh no you don't," Josh says.

He gets into the water fully clothed and holds me.

"You're the only family I have, Austria. We're going to be each other's family now. You have to stay with me."

MESSAGE

"When does it stop hurting?" I manage to make myself speak for the first time since I returned from the void.

The look of shock in Josh's eyes as he hears me brings a stab of guilt. I'm hurting him again when that's the last thing I want to do.

"I'm not going to lie. It never fully goes away, but as you live each day and find new joy, it slowly fades."

"It's not fair."

"Nothing is."

We hold each other for a long time without saying a word. Finally, as all of the rest of my physical feelings return to me, my stomach growls.

"Hungry?" Josh says and raises his eyebrows.

"Josh, your pajamas are soaked," I say. I'd forgotten he was fully clothed when he got in the tub. It just felt so comfortable in his arms.

"Yes, they are!" He stands and shakes like a wet dog.

I laugh. I didn't think that could be possible. He smiles in return and leans down, grabs the back of my neck, and kisses me. I grab his dripping clothes and pull him closer. Every feeling comes back to me. Maybe I can find new joy. I don't know how long we kiss. I don't care. I could stay here forever. Who cares if I turn into a prune? Eventually, he pulls away.

"You need some food."

"I'm okay. We can stay a little longer."

"Austria."

"Okay, okay."

He gets out, takes off his clothes, and hangs them on the shower rod. His muscles ripple with every move. He wraps a towel around his waist. What am I supposed to be doing again? He extends his hand to me. Oh yeah, I grab his hand. He helps me out of the tub and wraps me in a soft blanket. He kisses me again.

"Even utterly depressed you're beautiful, Austria."

"So are you."

Wait, that didn't come out right. Oh, who cares, he understands what I'm saying. He smiles at me and walks out. He returns with dry clothes for us both.

As we walk downstairs, I smell one of Tiff's special recipes to combat depression; blueberry, avocado, and tomato salsa with chips, fudge brownies, and strawberry banana protein shakes.

"Really, Tiff, are you pregnant or something? Do you normally mix foods like these together?" I hear Luke asking her.

"What if I *am* pregnant?" I hear her tease him. I wish we were already in the kitchen so I could see the look on his face.

"Well, uh, that, uh…" He's stumbling, and I'm smiling again.

"I'm not pregnant, silly. This is just a little soul food we enjoy when we're not feeling 100%. Is that okay with you, cowboy?" I can't believe I ever truly felt alone. Tiff is the best pseudo-sister a girl could have.

When we walk into the kitchen, they both stare at us.

"It's alive," Luke banters. "How are you doing, Austria?"

"I'm better."

He's beside me in a flash checking my vitals again. "Yes, you are." He smiles and hugs me.

"What did you do with her in that bathtub, Josh?" Tiff is now hugging me too. "Maybe you could give Luke a few pointers."

"Top secret. I could tell him, but then I'd have to kill him," Josh replies.

Luke fake-punches Josh in the arm. We all sit at the table and dig in. Even though Luke had mocked the food mix, he's enjoying it now. I notice my phone on the table.

It's blinking, indicating another message. I look at everyone, and they all look at me. Josh begins to move his arm but, before he can grab the phone, I get it. I unlock it and check the message. It's a message from my father being sent through my mother. And I'm no longer hungry. I get up, still staring at the screen, and begin to walk to my room. I hear one set of footsteps behind me. I know it's Josh, but I don't stop him. We're family. He can hear this. I have a feeling I'm going to need someone there to support me after the wave of emotion this is sure to bring.

"Austria,

Hi, darling. How are you doing? I hope you're all right. I wish I could be there to comfort you right now. I haven't figured everything out here, like how to communicate with you via a dream or vision. I've learned how to email from here. Your father had one more message to give you, but he ran out of time.

Love,

Mother"

"Austria,
I know you're upset, honey, but remember, I'll always love you. There's a reason why I have gone to such lengths to allow you to live a normal life and see the values in the world in which you live. There's also a reason why I have gotten you so involved with stopping our enemies. I didn't realize your mother was an Altered Helix until after you were conceived. You see, the committee in the Other World has been waiting for someone like you for years.

I wish Grandmother could tell you about it. Altered Helixes come from many countries around the world. A democratic vote determined that the royal leaders would be descendants of the first true-born Altered Helix. Austria, you are the first true-born. You're the first to be born from both Altered Helix parents. You're going to be the leader, but they want you to live a complete life prior to your final trip to the

Other World. Once you arrive to the Other World, you'll stop aging for long enough to rule.

I know this is a lot to take in right after going through such a loss, but it has to be said. Please don't worry. I know Josh is your family now and that your family may grow one day. I also know the last thing in the world you'll want to do is leave them. So I leave you with one blessing. The committee has worked to make a normal human become an Altered Helix without having to steal organs. This must remain a secret as we do not want our enemies to discover it. In all honesty, we would like to be rid of them when the Earth comes to an end, but that'll be something you and the committee can discuss. I tell you this so when it's your time to go you can bring your family with you if you wish. I'm giving you what I had wanted all along, honey, to have you. I love you. Take care.

Love,
Father"

My head is spinning. I don't know what to think of all this. Josh is holding me. By the lost look on his face, I can tell he read the message too.

MISSION

"You're what? Should we like call you princess now?" Ceresa's giving me a hard time after all I've lost.

"No, 'your highness' is more like it," Patrice adds as she flicks Ceresa on the arm with her hand.

I may be in pain, but these two still make me smile. I see where they're coming from now. They've been through this kind of pain. This is how they say they care. They do it by giving me a hard time instead of making me feel awkward and asking questions like, "Are you hanging in there?" I definitely like my pseudo-family right now.

"You can call me Princess Austria or your highness, whichever suits you," I answer with a sideways smile. "Just be sure to bow or curtsy when you do."

"Come on, your highness, let's go scare some people," Ethan says with a bow.

"I never thought I'd see you bow, man. Got to say, I don't mind it." Josh laughs.

"Whatever, Josh, You're not true royalty. You married in," Ethan counters.

"What's all this about married in?" Tiff's eyes bulge as she looks at Ethan.

Josh's face turns bright red. What in the world? We were just joking around. Tiff turns to Patrice and Ceresa, who are both nodding "yes" to her. "Yes" what? Everyone has become bizarre in my absence. What am I going to do with these fools? Don't they know how much we have on our plate? Tiff turns to me, and she has the biggest smile planted on her face.

"What? Why are you all looking at me like that? We have things to do."

"I think they can wait," Ethan says and then nudges Josh with his elbow.

Josh walks up to me with his hands in his pockets. Then he pulls one out. He's holding a small box. Oh. He gets down on one knee.

"Look who's bowing now." Ethan can't resist.

Josh just shakes his head. "Austria, I love you. You are my family. I want to be with you forever. Will you marry me?"

My eyes well up with tears. I hear the girls squeal. I'm happy and overwhelmed at the same time. I drop to my knees in front of him nodding my head yes, but I just can't get words out. Josh grabs me in a bear hug. I'm shaking with emotion. Even though I'm crying, he lifts my chin, smiles at me, and kisses me. He puts the ring on my finger. I look down and see it's a white gold Claddagh ring like I've always wanted, with hands holding a crowned heart; ironic that now I am "crowned." I hug him again. I want to stay in this embrace forever. Tiff grabs my hand and is inspecting the ring. Ethan jabs Josh in the side. We really are going to be a family.

Bill walks into the room and makes an announcement. "Customers will be here in an hour. We need to have everything set up and everyone in their places. What's all the commotion over here? Please tell me it isn't another disappearance."

He walks over to us, and Tiff holds out my hand. I watch Bill's eyes lighten when he sees what's going on. He smiles and hugs us both, Josh and I, together. Apparently, he approves of this union.

"Congratulations. Let me see if I have any treats in the storage room over here."

"Isn't it wonderful? I can't wait to tell my ...." Then I remember, I don't have anyone else alive to tell. Josh holds me tightly.

"Uh, Tiff, can you come over here and take a picture of Austria's ring and email it to her mother?" Josh asks the question that I'm too weak to ask.

Tiff comes over and takes the photo. She puts her hand on my cheek. She can see that tears of sadness have replaced the tears of joy. "Are you going to wear the ring with your costume?"

She's changing the subject. "Yeah, the ring fits perfectly. It won't fall off. Josh, how did you know my ring size?"

"Oh, a little birdie told me, and that little birdie's name is Tiff."

Now she's smiling, and my smile has returned too. I am a lucky girl. I have one hot fiancé and a dynamic best friend.

"Let's go scare some people," I almost scream.

##

After the haunted house closes, we head to Broadway Café. I had a blast scaring people, but now it's time for us to plan for our real jobs, saving Altered Helixes. We need more incriminating evidence, so we're going to set up another surveillance operation. We also need to get the legislation passed to change national human trafficking laws from not only protecting against sexual abuse and slavery, but also organ theft. We're going to travel all over to administer the serum that'll protect Altered Helix organs from being a viable option for our enemies. Then we'll need to corrupt the medical files. We have a lot to accomplish. Oh, and apparently I need to be planning a wedding too.

As we walk into the café, I imagine what our lives would be like if none of this existed. I would have my mother, father, and probably grandmother. People wouldn't be in danger apart from Earth fading. Would we be as close as we are, though? All of the trials we've been through have made us as tight knit as family in a very short time. I realize that I wouldn't change one thing as we stroll through the café, and more than a couple of pairs of eyes stare at us. I used to wonder what people thought of our different groups hanging out together, but now I truly do not care.

SURVEILLANCE

We located most of the Altered Helixes, and it just so happens that many of them reside in Memphis of all places. Josh and I arrive in Memphis on time. We sneak up the target building's emergency stairs and find the window for 3C. A team member from the Other World came to the apartment as a spirit, ahead of time when it was empty, and forced the window to unlock. Josh tests it. The window opens but with a pretty strong creak. Hopefully, Jason's a sound sleeper. We climb into his apartment. My heart's beating about twice as fast as it should. Thankfully, Jason's snoring. I can't get my hands to stop shaking when I open the box containing the syringe. Josh puts a hand on my arm and looks me in the eyes. He breathes in deeply and then out. I follow him but am still shaking. He'll have to administer the serum this time. I put the numbing agent on a cotton ball and hold it on Jason's elbow pit as lightly as I can. When enough time has passed, I test it. I flick the inside of Jason's arm and tense, expecting him to jump. He doesn't even flinch. Josh pokes him with the needle. We make it back outside safely and down the stairs undetected. Josh hugs me. We successfully administered serum to four Altered Helixes tonight. The sun will rise in an hour, so we head back to the hotel. We're not finished, but I feel better already.

"Hola! Quiet down." I can hear Patrice over the walkie-talkie. I completely missed the whole surveillance thing as I was with the medical corruption team last time. I'm still not able to participate directly in the surveillance, but I do get to hear them in action. Since Josh and I are in Memphis, we couldn't join them. We're travelling under the guise of a street kids' project, the government actually footing the hotel bill. We're able to listen into the surveillance via a walkie-talkie app on our phones. We sit in our hotel room and listen on edge. Even though I'm not there, I can completely imagine what their faces look like. Ethan must have a serious face; which is hard to picture on him. Patrice's face is full of concern. Camille and Emmitt are probably trying to decrease the tension with sarcasm, but it won't work.

"We've set up the microphones from the van so we'll pick up conversations inside the house. This bionic ear and booster sound amplifier is sweet," Emmitt says.

"You look ridiculous in those headphones, Emmitt." Camille's laughing.

"OUCH. Watch your volume," Emmitt complains.

"You better watch where you point that," Patrice instructs.

"Okay, Camille, are you set up for the emergency phone call if they bring in someone?" Ethan adds.

"Oh, they're talking, quiet down," Emmitt interrupts.

"I'm going to try to send what they're saying over Voxer so you can record it too," Patrice says to Josh and me.

"I can't believe it's happening next week," a man's voice says. It sounds a little different than Ethan's had. The sounds from the amplifier are a little fuzzy, but clear enough to make out the words. It also sounds eerily familiar, like it could belong to one of the guys who kidnapped me at the beginning of all this. How could he be out of jail already? He sounds pretty excited about whatever's going down. My father successfully stopped Adam, so what're they all pumped up about?

"I know. Can you believe we could have over a hundred?" another man says.

Over a hundred what?

"The commissioner opened up the old racetrack just for us. They think they're coming into the city from their small towns for a concert they won tickets to," the first man says. I scoot to the edge of my seat as he continues talking. "I'm glad we've had all this transplant practice. It's going to be hard to handle that many at a time."

"This is really going to shake things up a bit. I can't wait to rule the Other World. Ever think you'd be part of the group that leads an entire world?"

"I see Jerry's headlights. It looks like we get to practice one more time."

Well, this has been an insightful surveillance.

"Camille, make the emergency call. Maybe it's not too late to stop them," Ethan says.

"We got everything on record," says Emmitt.

"So did we," says Josh.

It's silent for a few minutes as the team waits to see what else the men have to say, but they're not talking.

I can hear sirens in the background. Aren't they supposed to silence those when there's a hostage? I hear commotion in the van.

"They're bailing. Why do the cops have their sirens on?" Camille takes the words right out of my mouth.

"Look, they're already rolling a gurney out. No black bag this time," Ethan says. In my head, I can see him pointing.

"They must have had it closer to the front door this time." Emmitt points out.

"Or maybe they moved it there to give them more time to get away?" Patrice adds.

Just then, there's a loud knock.

"What in the world?" Camille whispers.

"We know you're in there. We know you called the cops. What else have you been up to?" It's the man's voice from inside the house. Shoot, how did they find the van? I hear the sound of everyone rummaging around. Then someone yells, "Get going." Tires squeal. Camille yells a horror movie type of scream. Then I hear the shot.

LEGISLATION

"You have to keep driving. Get us out of here," Patrice says.

"It went clean through. I don't think it hit a major organ. I'm pretty sure he'd be bleeding more. Where's the closest hospital?" Camille asks.

"Seriously, it went all the way through. That's going to leave a mark," Emmitt says, and I can hear a mixture of panic and laughter in his voice.

"Guys, I'm having trouble losing them. Is there any way you can help get them off our tail?" Ethan sounds exasperated.

"I'll open the side window and throw things we don't need," Patrice answers.

Static breaks up our signal. Josh and I can't hear anything over it. Josh tries to make contact, but there's no answer. We wait a few minutes and then I try making contact.

"Patrice, are you guys okay?"

There's silence for a bit. I hear some shuffling around again.

"Whoever this is, we have your friends. If you want them back, you're going to have to turn in all the evidence you have on us. I know you must have some. Look at all the equipment in this van. Meet us tonight at 8:00 p.m. at Katarina's." It's the man's voice from the house. Crap, this isn't good.

"Okay, we'll do that, but one of our friends there is injured and can't wait that long. If he dies in your hands, we'll turn everything in to the police," I proclaim.

"Fine, lady, but then we'll have to kill your other three friends," he returns.

Shoot, I wasn't expecting that response. Josh grabs the phone.

"We'll see you at 8:00 p.m. at Katarina's." He hangs up.

I look at him furiously. If this were a cartoon, steam would be rolling out of my ears right now.

"Why did you hang up? Emmitt will die if he doesn't receive medical care soon."

"Austria, we're not waiting for the meeting at Katarina's. The bionic ear and booster sound amplifier that Emmitt's wearing is also tracking their location."

He pulls up a GPS-looking App on the phone, and I see a red dot blinking in Kansas City and a steady blue dot in Memphis.

"We're too far away to help him in the time he needs. How are we going to launch a rescue with half of our group away from headquarters?" Since we're on a mission to save lives now, we've named the haunted house headquarters.

"Bill and Ceresa are with Senator Justus right now. The senator has identified trustworthy police staff. We need to contact them and give them access to this tracker. Once they've saved our friends, we need to give them this evidence."

"You're right." I give him a hug full of the most hope I can muster. He makes the call.

Bill understands the urgency right away, and we have the police in pursuit of the van immediately. Then Bill puts us on speakerphone so we can join the meeting with Senator Justus. Ceresa is there too.

"I completely support you on this. Ceresa, you did a great job drafting this. I just wish there was a way I could get my fellow senators on board. But this will cost some money, you see, and right now everyone's trying to decrease expenses. It's what the voters want." This comes from who I assume is Senator Justus. She is amazing. I wish I were in the room with them.

"I thought we would just be modifying provisions relating to criminal law, and there wouldn't be that much cost involved," I say, hoping I'm not making a fool of myself in front of a senator.

"Well, it appears that a good number of the senators receive donations from this trafficking ring. So even though the costs are reasonable, the support isn't there because they'll lose those donations if they pass the bill. Looks like this group has coerced more than some of our police officers. There's really no telling how many pockets they've lined."

"Is there any way we could fluff the bill to look like it's for a different cause and just include this in a small section?" I ask, but then recall some politicians not passing a bill because of something small included within the text.

"We're pretty used to that, Austria. We have paid staff, and they're responsible for combing through every detail."

"Good. It took me a long time to draft this. I need to be spending my time preparing the new shelter instead of fluffing a bill," Ceresa complains.

"Well, we've been able to sway the vote before. Maybe we can do that again," Bill inserts.

"Yes, we did. Senator Justus, can you please help us by introducing this bill? We'll work on the committee it will be referred to," Josh says as he gives me a wink. He's right. We had help from the Other World for the homes for children bill. I'm sure they'll help us with this one too.

"I can do that. Thanks for dropping by. Good to talk with you. I'll have to be going now."

I hear Bill and Ceresa leave the room. Background noise continues for a couple minutes and then I hear car doors shut.

"Are you still there?" Bill asks.

"Yes," Josh and I say in unison. My face warms as I smile at him.

"A text message came through during our meeting with the senator. The police have the van. They've arrested the men who took it," Bill says.

I jump up and down and give Josh a hug.

"That's great, Bill."

Bill hesitates before responding, "You might want to head back as soon as you can. It's Emmitt. They're not sure he's going to make it."

Now I drop to my knees. Not someone else. I can't bear to lose anything more. Emmitt's too young. He can't die for our cause.

Josh holds me as he answers Bill. "We'll be there by this afternoon." Josh hangs up and grabs my face. I can see that he's holding back tears. His kiss is deep, communicating urgency and his determination to try to protect me.

DOMESTICATE

Walking into the hospital waiting room feels like being a prisoner on death row heading to the execution chamber. Josh holds my hand the entire way. Brittany and Landon are there in overalls and boots. They've been a lot of help to Ceresa building the new shelter. Now their eyes are swollen. We walk up to them and exchange hugs. Brittany's embrace is weak, like she doesn't have the strength to lift her arms. I see a woman I assume to be Emmitt's ma holding Camille. We head over to them and exchange hugs again. Camille's embrace is so strong that I feel as though she's using me to help her stand.

Luke and Tiff come up to us and lead us to some open chairs. "They aren't letting anyone visit Emmitt right now. He's in an operating room. The bullet hit a blood vessel. The blood seeped into his stomach, which is why Camille didn't see major bleeding. It took a while for the cops to locate the van and get Emmitt into the hospital. His heart was still beating upon arrival, so the original prognosis had been optimistic. That changed when they went to clean and suture the wound. They located the ruptured blood vessel and have been repairing, cleaning, and replenishing blood since," Luke informs us. We sit and wait patiently with everyone for the doctor.

As I look at Camille, I imagine what it would be like in her shoes. We're both Altered Helixes with partners that have normal DNA. They're putting themselves at risk for us. I see the pain, fear, and guilt in her eyes. They mirror my own emotions. Should we be handling this all by ourselves? I mean, we're the ones that heal faster. We're also the targeted ones, or at least we were. Now I'm beginning to wonder if we have broadened the target to our entire group since we've been fighting against the human trafficking ring. I can't believe I allowed the ones I care about to be dragged into this mess. Maybe they dragged themselves in when they came to save me. Here I am alive, and Emmitt's possibly going to die in my place. I can't take it. I stand. I can't just sit here and wait.

"Would any of you like something to eat or drink?" I ask the group.

"Here, grab some waters and crackers. Everyone is in need of both," Bill hands me a five. Maybe I can get some cups from the coffee area. Josh and Ceresa stand to join me.

"We can help you carry everything," Ceresa says.

It feels a little better doing something. We're silent as we walk to the refreshments room.

"Ceresa, how's the shelter coming along?"

"Oh, it's tremendous. We have six of the apartments renovated. Thank you so much for hooking us up with that home improvement gal—she's innovative and decorates each one so that it looks like a home. So many shelters feel like boxes, or as if we're animals being kept in a cage. They don't have enough money to put more than the basic necessities in. With her fund-raising, she's able to do much more. With the bill passing, we're going to be able to take over another rundown building and set it up as a training facility. I want to get as many street kids back into stable living as I can. It's slow going, but we're making considerable changes, Austria"

"That sounds remarkable. Can I stop by and see one of the apartments sometime?"

"Of course you can. What's your schedule like?"

"Well, we left Memphis early to come and see Emmitt. We need to get back. I'm not sure how we're going to administer all the serum we need to in time," Josh tells Ceresa.

"Jack and Lea are looking for things to do," she tells him.

I grit my teeth. I know we need the help, but I don't want to get anyone else involved in this fiasco. I especially don't want to get our youngest involved. I feel protective as a mama bear of Jack.

"Hey, let's get back. I don't want to miss what the doctor has to say," I interrupt.

We head back to the waiting room. Ceresa and Josh both carry six cups of water each. I was only able to get five packets of crackers, but I'm not sure many of us are going to be eating so it should be enough. I give Bill his change and he nods at me.

I remember when I first met Emmitt. He was the one who faked a heart attack when Ceresa surprised his group. I remember thinking how bright his smile was. His dimples definitely help it stand out. I remember Brittany's, Landon's, Camille's, and Emmitt's story of spending an evening as street kids. Emmitt was the one who snuck into a bar to get them water. This group of college graduates struggled economically but grew spiritually. They're people I admire.

They're like my siblings, and now my brother is in the hospital. "Please let him be okay," I chant over and over in my head.

Finally, a doctor enters the waiting room. He has a serious look on his face, but I can't tell if this means the news is good or bad. He just looks deep in concentration. He walks over to Emmitt's ma and begins talking. I can't hear him, so we try to get closer. After two steps, Emmitt's ma leaps out of her chair and hugs the doctor. I smile as this must mean good news.

"My baby is okay. Emmitt's going to live."

We all run in to give her a hug. She raises her hands and waves them at the doctor. "Can I see my boy?"

"Of course. He's still in recovery, so he'll be very groggy. He needs rest so keep it short."

VOYAGE

"I know the rules. I spy with my little eye something blue," Lea says.

"Is it the water tower at the top of that hill?" Jack asks pointing to said water tower.

"Yes, good job."

They've been playing this game for the last hour. I know we're saving money by driving, but I don't know how much more I can take. There was no way we could talk the government into allowing four people on this paid trip. Lea called a cousin who lives in Memphis, and we're crashing with him. Guess I'm paying for a free place to stay by putting up with the childish road games.

"So, has the numbing agent worked on everyone so far? What's the plan if it doesn't work or if they wake up?" Jack asks.

"Kid, if the numbing agent doesn't work, they're more than likely going to wake up. If they wake up, you had better run," Josh answers.

"What if they catch us? I don't want Jack taken again," a concerned Lea says.

"A spirit from the Other World will be watching each time and will intervene if that ever happens. You'll need to be mindful of where your exit is at all times, pay attention and be prepared," I answer. Now I wish Lea had been part of our self-defense training.

"Could you two be quiet for a little while? I'm going to call back home and see how things are going," Josh announces.

He puts it on speakerphone so we can all hear.

Bill answers. "Hi, kids, how's the drive?"

"Long," I say. "How's Emmitt?"

"He's recovering quickly. He'll be out of the hospital in a couple days. He still needs bed rest for a couple weeks while everything heals. Then he'll be a hundred percent."

"That's great news. Any luck on shutting down the racetrack?"

"We were able to change the commissioner's mind on that one. We've also acquired the list of invitees to the event. And the list of event employees. That list was turned into the police along with the recording. We've made great headway."

"Wow, that's much better than expected. Thank you." I can't believe how lucky we are. First, Emmitt's going to be completely fine and then we completely botch those idiots' plans and land them on the path to jail.

"Tell Emmitt we miss him and hope he has a quick recovery," Jack and Lea say in unison. Even though they can be a little annoying, they're still cute.

"Will do. You kids be safe now." Is that a hint of anxiety I hear in Bill's voice?

"Thanks, Bill. We will." Josh hangs up the phone. Now it's time for us to train Jack and Lea. Then we'll separate. We have seven more Altered Helixes in Memphis. This is going to be a long weekend.

##

Jack and Lea climb the apartment emergency stairs with ease. Jack's able to open the window; that doesn't squeak. We all enter quietly. We have blueprints of every place and review them prior to entry. Not a sound is made as we tiptoe to the bedroom. Then I hear a hiss. I jump. Elizabeth's cat doesn't seem to like us. We're within view of her now. She hasn't stirred. I can hear Jack breathing hard and fast. We walk into the room. Elizabeth's face glows red in the light of her alarm clock. Jack fumbles trying to open the syringe case. Lea takes it from him and opens it. Jack takes the cotton ball with numbing agent and holds it on Elizabeth's insertion point. We watch the red digits. After a minute has passed, Jack removes the cotton ball. Lea inserts the needle and serum. Josh and I watch Elizabeth's face. She twitches, as if someone tickled her nose with a feather. Lea's done and quickly pulls the syringe away. Just in time because Elizabeth sneezes. Her hands automatically fly up toward her face. We all freeze. Elizabeth rolls over, away from us, and I hear her breathing return to its original pace. That was close. We turn around and exit as silently as we entered. The cat must've hid from us because I don't see it again.

"That was great. We got to watch you both apply numbing agent and administer serum last time, but that's nothing compared to actually doing it ourselves," Jack exclaims in the car.

We drop them off at Lea's cousin's car. They're going to administer the serum to two more Altered Helixes, and we'll roll through another three. We are to call each other if we run into any trouble, otherwise we'll meet at Lea's cousin's place at 5:00 a.m.

##

During Josh and my last Altered Helix inoculation, I feel my body dragging. I can't remember when we had a full night of sleep. I can't wait for this to be over. Hopefully, we can get some rest before we head out again. We've done this so many times now that our movements feel mechanical. We enter the building and head to the room. Josh almost trips on the Altered Helix's boots on the way to the bed. We freeze and the adrenaline wakes us up. The man remains asleep on his bed, so we continue. As I hold the cotton ball to the man's arm, he flinches.

The next move he makes takes us both by surprise. Before we know it, he has a gun held to Josh's temple. Josh doesn't move. His eyes are wide. The man sits up and assesses us.

"Please, don't shoot. We're just trying to protect you from a human trafficking ring," I plead desperately with the man.

"What in the world are you two kids doing? What's in that syringe?"

"It's a long story, but keep the syringe and have it tested. What she says is true; we're only here to save you." Josh has regained his usual composure.

"Don't tell me what to do, boy." That's when I notice a star tattoo on the guy's shoulder.

"You have a tattoo just like my father's," I breathe out, amazed.

"Who's your dad, kid?"

"Brennan Andrews." I look into the man's eyes, hoping for understanding.

"No kidding! Brennan and I were in the Olympics together. Never did find out what happened to him." Josh hands him the syringe, and the man lowers his gun. I'm able to relax a little.

He walks us over to his kitchen and invites us to have a seat at his small but neat table. He offers us a drink, but we both just ask for a glass of water. As he pours some liquor for himself, I begin to unravel the story about my father and why we're there. My emotions do a complete one-eighty as he spills details about my father I never knew, like his record-beating sprint time. By the end of our conversation, he's administered the serum to himself. I find out his name is Daniel Browning. He even comes around so far as to offer a hand in our movement. When Josh tells him we must leave for our rendezvous, I'm relieved, as I'm almost delirious with lack of sleep. Daniel gives us his number, and we give him ours.

The realization of what could've happened doesn't hit until we're back in the car. As Josh drives I begin shaking so hard I can't stop. Josh has to pull over to reassure me that everything's okay and that he's not going anywhere. We just can't be doing this all on our own. I need to consult with my mother, but I think with the identities of

Altered Helixes known and with the help of the Other World's shadows, we should be able to recruit many more. It's time to set our secrets aside. Time to initiate new plans.

At 5:15 a.m. Jack and Lea have still not returned to her cousin's. Josh and I are pacing back and forth in the kitchen.

"Have you tried calling them again?" I ask anxiously.

"Yes, Austria, I'll send a text to Jack and Lea now."

The phone rings, and Josh puts it on speaker.

"Hi, Josh and Austria, sorry we're running late. We should be there in ten minutes." It's Jack, and I can breathe again.

"What happened?" Josh asks.

"Nothing happened. The serum applications went as planned without a hiccup," Jack answers.

Josh lets out a frustrated sigh.

"What he means is that everything went according to plan until we got lost on the way to my cousin's," Lea fills in the gaps.

"Why aren't you using GPS?" I ask.

"That's exactly what I told him." I can hear Jack and Lea whisper, bickering in the background. "He claimed he had the whole layout memorized. Which he did, I was really impressed, until it came time to head back."

"Not exactly a good time to be showing off for the lady. See you soon and turn on the damn GPS," Josh says and hangs up. I believe if he heard a rebuttal from Jack, he would find a way to reach his hand through the phone and give Jack a good slap upside the head.

"Hey, at least all the serum was administered." I try to point out the positive. Josh grabs my hand, sighs, and sits next to me. The kiss he plants on me after that makes me forget about everything.

CORRUPTION

Jack and Lea walk in just as we get Tiff and Luke on Walkie-Talkie, and my blood's able to take in oxygen. The sunrise shining behind them blinds me for a second when they open the door. The scene of them in the doorway with the sun at their backs reminds me of an old western. Jack sticks his chin up and walks with his shoulders back like he just made a game-winning touchdown. Lea slaps his arm and rolls her eyes. It's as if they're an old married couple. Maybe some people are made and molded for one another since the beginning of time.

"Hi. How's Memphis?" It's Luke.

"We're kicking butt and taking names," Jack exclaims proudly, and Josh shakes his head side to side.

"All right, we're getting ready to exit the car and enter the medical research site so we'll have you muted, but you'll be able to hear us." I can tell Tiff is in game mode.

I can hear their footprints as they approach the building. The alarm rings for just a second before the code is punched in. Instead of the clicking of keys, I hear the tapping of fingers. This alarm must have a touch screen. This is the last medical research facility that we showed as pinpointing our kind of DNA. Once Tiff and Luke are done here, they can update the Helix Flat File, and our current mission will be complete. We're going to be administering serum and updating the file for years, but at least now all of the information our enemies have will be wiped.

I hear the clicking of keys as Luke begins finding the Altered Helix files. He's going to change them to depict disease indications and possible cures so they'll be hidden with other files. I even hear the sliding glass door to the refrigerated room the cultures are stored in. Tiff must be using the syringe to add foreign matter to the Altered

Helix samples. I picture her as methodic as when she's memorizing orders made at a restaurant table.

Noises continue as they go about their work. It seems to take forever; the second hand of a watch moving painfully slow. After the last Walkie-Talkie experience and what Josh and I just went through, I'm very anxious. I begin biting my nails, which I normally don't do. Finally, I hear Tiff.

"All targeted tubes now have foreign matter in them."

"Babe, you're definitely not meant for the medical world." Oh Luke, you shouldn't have said that.

I hear footsteps and then laughing. Tiff has gotten to Luke. I haven't actually heard him laugh that much. It even sounds like giggling.

"Stop it," he manages. Tiff must be tickling him. How does she always find peoples' weak spots?

"Fine, but don't knock my slang medical terms."

"We're accessing the Helix Flat File now," Luke tells us.

I hear more clicking of keys. Then I hear a mouse click. With every click, I see an enemy in handcuffs. With every click, I see a target removed from a friend. With every click, my blood is able to flow a little easier.

"We're almost finished." I take a breath of relief with Luke's words.

That's when I hear a commotion like something was just knocked over. My memory reels back to when Josh broke his arm. I'm still amazed he's been able to help with so much one-handed. I wait for someone to say they accidentally ran into something, but it's silent for a bit. Then I hear clanging and footsteps. I can hear heavy breathing like someone running. I hear car doors slam and tires peel out. The oxygen is slowly removing itself from my bloodstream.

"Shoot, they're chasing us. How many are there, Tiff?"

"Crap, there are at least three cars tailing us. Can't you make this thing go any faster?"

I hear the acceleration of the engine. Tiff, my best friend and pseudo-sister, is being chased by three freaking cars. How in the world did it come to this? Neither Tiff nor Luke are Altered Helixes. Why are they getting the most heat? Is it because their actions are essential to this mission? I don't know. How would our enemies know? I imagine Luke and Tiff holding hands, running from a pursuit like Thelma and Louise. Well, of course, instead of being chased by the cops, they're being pursued by criminals.

"Were you able to update the data on the Helix Flat File to show the serum has been administered?" Josh asks the question I want an answer to, but I cannot focus through my worry for Tiff.

"Yeah, we got it. It's saved globally so they can't change it," Luke answers.

"That's awesome. You're a real genius," Jack says.

"Yeah, now if I can just figure out how to lose this tail."

I can hear the workings of the car. It sounds like the four-wheel drive has been turned on, and they're off-road; mud flying from the wheels. Again I am repeating to myself, "Please let them be okay."

"Tiff, I know I'm awful at expressing my feelings, but I love you." I hear Luke kiss Tiff. I'm not sure if he's kissing her hand or her cheek. I remember his ruffled hair the first morning after they spent a night together. They were adorable standing side by side in the kitchen.

"I love you too, Luke. Austria, if you can still hear us, I love you." I hear a crash of twisted metal and exploding plastic. Then we lose connection. If there is any oxygen in my blood, I do not feel it now.

COMPLETION

I fall into the state of shock instantaneously. This time, a black sheet is pulled over my face. I don't remember leaving the kitchen or rising from my chair. I don't remember any "I spy" games during the road trip back. I can't even recall if I went to the bathroom or ate any food. All I can remember is thinking, "It's my fault." The only reason Tiff had been involved was because of me. The void I feel is not like losing a parent but losing a sibling. The feeling that I could have avoided this overwhelms me. I wake in the haunted house inventory room. My friends are walking all around me in a hurry. They all seem to have something to do. There are dresses, makeup, and hair products everywhere. The door to the room opens.

Tiff walks in. "Wait, what?" Is this Heaven? Will my father and grandmother come through that door next? She walks up to me and gives me a hug. I tremble, not wanting to wake from this dream.

"Austria, hon, are you going to wake up for your big day? No one wants a zombie for a bride, even if the wedding is in a haunted house. We all worked really hard putting this together while you were in Memphis. You've already told me everything you want, and I've followed it to a T."

"Tiff." I touch her face to see if it's real. "You're really here." Tears unlike any I've experienced before sting my eyes. I didn't know tears could burn so. Tiff gets out a handkerchief and dabs around my eyes.

"Yes, I'm here. Luke and I escaped the chase. We communicated that to you right away, but you'd gone into a state of shock. You've been in a state of shock for two days now, Austria"

"I thought you were dead. I don't know what happened. The thought of losing you just made me break."

"Well, you didn't lose me, and I don't plan on you losing me for a long time, so snap out of it."

She walks to the closet and grabs a large sack covering something on a hanger. She moves over to me and lifts the sack revealing a dress. It's my mother's wedding dress. Yes, it is vintage style. This style is currently in. It's a princess style with Irish lace on the chest, but not touching the neck and just barely folding over the shoulders. Instead of the flowery lace of many vintage dresses, this one has curlicues, which are all the rage, and they've dyed the lace black as I requested. Some people would be petrified to wear their mother's dress, but I'm stoked. Not only is the dress gorgeous, but it means that I get to have a piece of her with me on my big day. Everyone says weddings bring tears of joy to many people, and I used to never get it, but now I do.

Picturing my mother in that dress holding my father's hand causes a small flood to emerge right below my eyelids.

Lea comes over and gives me a hug. "Glad you're among the living again. Let me just touch up your makeup a little."

She's dabbing so many things on my face that I can't even keep up. Tiff and Patrice help me get into the dress. Ceresa and Camille roll over a full-length mirror. Oh my, who is that woman in the mirror? She looks mature, like she's experienced the world. She has a strength behind her eyes that mine never have had. It reminds me of someone. It reminds me of my mother raising me half all on her own, applying Band-Aids on every wound, and running every project I forgot at home up to school.

"You guys really planned the entire thing, so I don't have to?" I ask all of my dear friends.

"We did. I hope you're not mad at us," Tiff exclaims.

"No, this is fabulous. Thank you."

We all come in for a group hug. As we walk to the main entrance, I become dizzy with emotion. I feel like I've reached bottomless lows and unreachable highs throughout this journey. I can't wait to see Josh. I remember when I gave him a peck kiss to show dominance in the beginning. A smile washes over me. The electric buzz I felt as our fingertips met at the rollaway rack of costumes has never vanished. I tingle every time we touch. He has gone to great lengths to be there for me. We're going to become legal family today.

Before we emerge from the hallway, I see white folding chairs adorned with satin and black ties. They're all lined up on both sides of the aisle. The light emerging from the stained-glass windows overhead and at the sides gives a moonlike glow. Each row of chairs has a round white floral decoration hanging from black iron posts. In front of all of the chairs is the beautiful organ. I see all of my friends and pseudo-family walk in front of me. Some take a seat and some head up the curved staircase on the side that leads to the front to stand next to us. Josh is next to the organ, kicking his feet at the ground just as he was when we first met. He looks at me and smiles nervously. I smile back. The look of relief that washes over him makes my heart skip a beat. I must have scared him yet again with my comatose state.

Bill waits for me behind the chairs. He extends his arm for me to take so I can be escorted down the aisle. I smile at him, then look above. *Father, I miss you. You understand, right?* I take Bill's arm and begin the march forward. That's when I hear the music; it's my mother playing the piano. I would recognize her playing style anywhere. I almost choke up when I the wedding march begins, but I can't stop smiling. How did they get this recording? Did she leave it before she left? The closer we get, the more complete I feel. Bill gives my hand to Josh. He takes it and peck kisses me on the cheek. He points me towards the organ bench and waves. There's a laptop on it. My mother's image is on it too, and she's waving back from behind a piano. The music was live. I let the tears flow now. I break away from Josh and run to the computer.

"Is it really you? How's this happening?"

"Hi, darling, congratulations."

"We figured out how to Video Chat from this world and the Other World, Austria," Josh says. "Your mother can see us get married. She can see our babies being born. She can view every big experience."

I hug Josh. I don't know how he did it. I don't know how he knew I needed it, but he did. This is just icing on the cake. Josh is the man I want to spend the rest of my life with.

"Love you," I say as I brush my tears away. Mom's doing the same.

"Love you too, baby," Mom says.

Josh and I scale the stairs. The bannister is encased in black ribbon. We exchange vows and kiss. As we walk to the reception,

I look at our pseudo-family and smile. We've all accomplished so much. Bill and Ceresa have a home for street kids to run. Tiff will make it in acting and put her talent to full-time use. Luke and Tiff are about to get engaged. I know because he asked for my approval before we left town. He'll be a doctor and she a happy wife. Ethan and Patrice will still roam the streets but should have more safe-homes than before. Camille and Emmitt will enjoy a happy life together. One they will never take for granted after the scare of almost losing him. Brittany and Landon will be there to help them along. Jack and Lea can be kids for a little bit longer. All of us have accomplished so much while saving the Altered Helixes. Yes, while the haunted house did bring us many scary moments, without it we would have none of these miracles and joys to celebrate. And if you ever wake up because you feel the poke of a needle in your arm, don't be afraid, because it's me or one of my friends administering a serum, and you are an Altered Helix.

ACKNOWLEDGMENTS

The transformation this novella has been through would not have been possible without many people. There's no way I can name them all but I'd like to give it a try. They know how hard I've worked and how many years I've dedicated to books. First, I would like to thank the readers. You breathe life into books and for that I will be ever thankful. Next, I would like to thank the professionals that helped me trudge through this thing called publishing: everyone at Hypothesis Productions, Ben Furnish, Carol Cartaino, Dr. Luthi, Michael Neff, Brendan Deneen, Randi Hacker, the Lawrence SCBWI Critique Group, Amy Brewer, Patty Carothers, and Rick Miles. Next, I would like to thank my friends who saw me through dark times and helped me celebrate the good times too: Shana Bartlett, James Young, Miranda Nichols, Amy Garton, Stacked Book Club, Sarah Smith, and Cathy Wissing. Finally, I would like to thank my family for putting up with me: Nate, Ethan, Jenna, Vic Hurlbert, Debra Scarborough, Cassandra Hurlbert, Victor Hurlbert, Vondell Neill, and Peggy Hurlbert. If I inadvertently left someone off the list please let me know so I can add them to the next book.

ABOUT THE AUTHOR

Stephanie Hansen's short story, Break Time, and poetry has been featured in Mind's Eye literary magazine. The Kansas Writers Association published her short story, Existing Forces, appointing her as a noted author. She has held a deep passion for writing since early childhood, but a brush with death caused her to allow it to grow. She's part of an SCBWI critique group in Lawrence, KS and two local book clubs. She attends many writers' conferences including the New York Pitch, Penned Con, New Letters, All Write Now, Show Me Writers Master Class, BEA, and Nebraska Writers Guild conference as well as Book Fairs and Comic-Cons. She's a member of the deaf and hard of hearing community. https://www.authorstephaniehansen.com/

Don't miss books by Stephanie Hansen
https://www.authorstephaniehansen.com/